The Indifferent Stars

Peter Traynor

© Peter Traynor, 2020: The author retains the right to be identified as the author of this work

Excerpt from the book

'Hello?' I say, peering over at a pair of legs protruding from the cabin of a trawler that is bobbing in the harbour. The legs remain determinedly silent.

'Hello?' I ask again.

'Howdy up there.' a reply. The legs shrimp away from the cabin, and a body appears on deck, with a worn, bearded face: thin, unsmiling but not unfriendly.

'What can I do for yer?' he asks, eyebrows raised.

'I've been told you run tours to Hudson Bay. I'd like to book myself on one if I may?'

What readers are saying about the book

"A miniature masterpiece of hope and new life. There's a wonderful generosity about this journey, where warmth and joy emerge in and from the coldest of places." *Andrew Edwards, BBC Radio Leeds*.

"Delightful and engaging tale of adventure, loss and rediscovery."

"Beautifully wrapped wisdom and humour."

"The writer paints the environment so well, you could be there."

"A heartfelt delight…I hope there is more on the way!"

In memory of my dad

Michael Traynor

Missed every day

Dear Monica, dear Matthew,

I am going away. Your mum and I always planned to do a round-the-world trip, and I intend to honour that. I have decided not to come back. Please do not be angry, I'm lonely at home on my own, and bored. It is for the best. Know that I love you both, and of course George, and little Sammy. Let them remember me as I am now. The house is taken care of. You will be getting a call from my solicitor soon, please be kind to him.

I love you all very much

Dad xxx

THE VOYAGE STARTS...

Losing someone you love really hurts. It's not like in the movies, where people just seem to forget about things after a few days. Well in some ways, it is too much like the movies. It's bad enough to find myself walking down the street, unable to stop crying, but then to suddenly get the sense of being in one of the hundreds of sad films I've watched over a lifetime makes it even worse, and somehow diminishes an already diminishing experience. It is human to be self-conscious I suppose, even at the worst of times, but it is also irritating; I do not need my life to be sound-tracked.

In other ways, losing someone you love is definitely not like in the movies. It hurts. It really hurts like nothing else hurts. It saps the marrow from your bones and leaves you shrivelled, empty, and bereft of hope and strength. I shattered my ankle some years ago whilst playing football. The broken bone punched right through the skin. The crack was so loud that everyone on the pitch heard it, stopped what they were doing and gawped at me until the ambulance came and carried me off. That hurt. But it was nothing compared to the pain of losing Laura.

How do you cope with the death of someone you have loved for over forty years? Where does everything go? The laughter, the tears, the funny moments, so many little annoyances. They just disappear, like treasured possessions from a burgled house, never to be seen again. How does a person just disappear like that? Why give someone such a wonderful gift of love, only to take it away? It makes no sense.

So, I've decided to go away. In a universe that makes no sense, anything is possible. I am old, tired, and fed up. I have always wanted to see the great Hudson Bay, a vast expanse of water in the arctic wilderness. If God exists anywhere on this planet, I have always thought it would be there. Maybe I will find him and ask him what he thinks he's playing at. After that, well it doesn't matter really. First, however, I wish to see the world. Laura and I planned to do this together, but now I go alone.

THREE MONTHS LATER...

Montreal is a pleasant change of pace, and climate, from the rigours of Hong Kong. It is chilly but bright and friendly. I went out in the evening and got some steak and chips, Quebecois style. The hotel is not as cosy as it looked on the internet, in fact it's quite cold. I complained twice to the receptionist, but he just pursed his lips and shrugged, and said there was nothing he could do. After a bit more complaining I got an extra blanket and a free whisky out of it.

The children will have received the letters by now. I do hope they are not too upset. Sod them, they never come to see me anyway, and when they do they just sit around waiting to leave again. And they never tidy up after themselves. I will miss the grandchildren though. It is for the best this way, at least they will remember me fit and strong; if they remember me at all.

I go this morning to the harbour to book a boat. The first person I speak to, a young man named Jacques, looks at me as if I am crazy, and asks if I had misread the scale on my map. It turns out I had. Jacques suggests I just fly straight there, but if I was truly committed to my (patently absurd) plan, he thought I should at the least charter a small plane out to Labrador and find a boat to take me from there – it would save a couple of weeks. Seems like a good idea. I must confess, although this is, or should, be the final part of my trip, I haven't really planned it as well as the rest. I am just hoping that things will take their course. Let's see how it goes.

I take Jacques' advice and go to the airport. It is a single building with a small airstrip. Three hours later I'm flying over sheets and shards of frozen rock in a battered old Cessna Skyhawk that has seen better days. The pilot is a middle-aged woman who talks a lot but never seems to have flown before.

I touch down in Hopedale late evening, and head to the only hotel in town, if you can call it a town, it seems more like an expanded truck stop. The roads out here are huge. The hotel is quiet, a few oil workers on their way to somewhere, and the landlady. Everyone speaks quietly. I finish with a nice glass of whiskey and sneak off to bed. I have been advised to look for a boat called Santiago. I tingle with anticipation. I miss Laura.

DOWN AT THE HARBOUR

'Hello?' I say, peering over at a pair of legs protruding from the cabin of a trawler that is bobbing in the harbour. The legs remain determinedly silent.

'Hello?' I ask again.

'Howdy up there.' a reply. The legs shrimp away from the cabin, and a body appears on deck, with a worn, bearded face: thin, unsmiling but not unfriendly.

'What can I do for yer?' he asks, eyebrows raised.

'I've been told you run tours to Hudson Bay. I'd like to book myself on one if I may?'

I cast my eyes over the boat. It is a dirty white colour and has a large cabin with portholes dotted around it. Splashed across the vessel's prow in pale blue paint is written 'Santiago'. It does not fill me with optimism.

'Certainly, sir, let me have a look at the book,' he says.

He stands, a wiry old man, with grey straggly hair run yellow in places, held back from a wrinkled forehead by a faded blue bandana. His eyes meet mine for a second as he scans his ledger.

'When are y' hoping to set off sir?' he asks.

'Any time soon.'

'As luck would have it, we've a tour setting off tomorrow, and we can fit in you in. You'll even have yer own room.' His voice brightens as he says this as if telling me something about which I should be very excited.

'Brilliant, thank you. How much will it cost though?' I ask.

'Oh don't worry 'bout that sir, y' can talk about that in the morning with the captain, just be here for seven, we set off at eight.'

A SPECIAL TOUR

The morning is bright and clear when I make my way back to the harbour. It has been a lonely journey so far. I expected a small crowd of holiday-makers waiting at the to take the trip. We would be muted at first, but as the trip progressed, we would open up, learn something, bond and make lasting friendships. Instead, it is just me and my suitcase. Approaching the boat, I am greeted by the old sailor I spoke to yesterday.

'Howdy again. Are yer ready?' he asks, bright-eyed.

'Yes, just waiting to see the captain,' I say.

'Well a pleasure to meet yer sir, I'm the captain, but you can call me Ned,' he replies.

'Oh, you didn't say you were the captain yesterday,' I ask, perplexed.

'I was the mechanic yesterday sir, not much good at multi-tasking.' He says this whilst hoisting a heavy sack onto the boat.

'Right. Well, how much do you charge for this tour?'

'It'll be three hundred dollars to get there, five hundred if yer wantin' to come back. That includes food and board.'

'I think I just want to go one way actually.'

He stops and looks at me, eyes narrowed.

'Are y' sure sir? There's not much to do out there.'

'Yes that's fine, just one way, for now, thank you. If I change my mind, I will let you know.'

'Ok sir, I'd best show y' to yer quarters then,' he says, carrying another sack. 'I've given y' the best cabin. Have y' had breakfast yet? Yup, good, well we'll set off at eight. Are y' British?' he asks as he hops nimbly over the gap between the boat and the jetty. I see a flash of slate-grey water through the gap. It looks cold.

'Yes I am,' I reply.

'Where from?'

'Somerset.'

'Well we do some great British food on board, and we're loaded up with bacon, eggs, bread, tea, you name it. The cook is real talented, and you won't want for anything, I guarantee.'

He seems jaunty as he says this. I have rather more trepidation. Nonetheless, I step, nervously over the gap, my right foot testing the solidity of the vessel before I hop, somewhat less nimbly than my new companion, onto the boat.

ROAST SWAN

Morning has long broken by the time we set off, and dawn is a yellow-tinted memory. The day is cold and clear and the boat purrs along nicely. It is a comforting sound, that gentle thrum; it goes right through the chest. We hug the coastline. Further out the sea is breath-taking; obsidian cliffs rise and fall like mountains of glass. It seems to call us, tempting us out into its boundless expanse, mocking our smallness and timidity.

I haven't really thought this through. I imagined I might die out here, in a cold and savage place, but whilst it is certainly cold, it is not very savage. There might be some fierce beasts along the way, but I didn't really imagine myself being eaten. I just thought I might somehow fade away, cease to be.

Life is not fair. In the olden days, when you got old, you would be left out for the wolves, or the lions. What a way to go, like a wildebeest – blood, guts, teeth everywhere. Failing that, if you got too old to look after yourself, or you started complaining too often, I'm sure someone would eventually draw the short straw and sneak up on you in the middle of the night, and *shttt*, end of problem. I keep waiting for someone to come and *shttt* me, but they never do.

We chug along. Ned faces forwards, his wind-burnt cheeks and blue-grey eyes, the colour of the sea, always searching ahead.

'So what brings y' out here sir?' he asks.

'I came out here to die,' I say, only realising how strange that sounds after I have said it out loud for the first time.

'Have y' got somethin' in mind?' he asks, eyes fixed on where we are going.

'No not really, I just thought it might happen.'

'Y' don't look near death,' he says, glancing briefly in my direction as if to check the accuracy of what he has just said.

'I'm older than I look. I've had a good life, but I'm just about ready to go.'

'Seems a shame to give it up,' he says, still looking ahead, 'but not my place to question. The sea's calm, the boat's in good fettle, that's about all I ask for.'

'Where are we stopping for lunch?' I ask, 'and where are the other passengers - I thought you said yesterday there was a tour?'

'Not sure yet, sir, let's see how the weather holds. This is a tour, a one-man special, just for you. Yer very lucky!' he says, his tone rising.

My heart sinks a little.

'Ah ok,' I say, 'so when was the last time you did a tour then?'

'What year is it again?' he asks, seemingly genuine. I tell him.

'Is it really? Well, there were some folk out here from Japan a few years back.'

'Bloody hell. So what do you do in between tours?'

'Plenty. Take workers out to the rigs and the big hydro-station. Freight stuff around the coast. Folks are always want something moving somewhere, and I'm yer man. There's too much work to be truthful, not had a day off in ten years.'

His face furrows as he says this, clearly this is a man not accustomed to a great deal of leisure time. It must be nice to be in demand.

We stop for lunch in a little harbour. Three forlorn-looking houses perch precariously, at the bottom of a sheer rock wall. A winding and rather impossible-looking road runs up the wall, to god knows where. Ours is the only vessel in the harbour, though an imposing concrete jetty hints of busier days gone by.

I seek out the boat's dining room, hungry from all the fresh air. It is a mean little affair. A plastic table is pinned to the floor, surrounded by benches with maroon covers, out of which poke bits of yellowed foam.

Ned emerges from the kitchen in a cook's apron.

'So you're the cook as well then?' I ask, not at all surprised by this turn of events.

'Yes sir,' he says chirpily.

'I might have known,' I say, 'you spoke very highly of yourself yesterday.'

'Well sir, many years ago I cooked for a Saudi prince.'

'Really?'

'Yup.'

'So what did you cook him?'

'Well sir, he had a most diverse appetite. Sometimes he just loved fried chicken wings. Other times he loved a bit of Baba Ghanouj, that's a traditional Persian dish. Made with eggplant.'

'Sounds fairly dull for a prince,' I say, unimpressed.

'We did banquets too. They sure love their banquets, "abundance" they call it. Always cook more 'n they would eat in a year.

'That sounds like a lot of fried chicken!'

'Weren't just chicken. One time we roasted a swan. Straight out o' the cookbook of Louis the fourteenth,' he says, his eyes glazing slightly as he reaches back in time to a fond memory.

'Swan. What does that taste like?' I ask, intrigued.

'Not too good t' be truthful. In fact, after we sewed the roasted carcass back into its skin, feathers and all, we added duck meat to it, so that folk could pick bits of it off as they went along. By the end of the night, that was one sorry looking swan.'

'Well I never. So what are we having then?' I ask.

'Smoked mackerel,' he replies, flatly.

'Oh.'

'Well s'cuse me sir, but you ain't no Saudi prince.'

'Haha yes very true. Smoked mackerel will be just fine.'

The mackerel is better than fine, it is delicious, and served with sliced fried potatoes, rye bread, and marmalade. Afterwards, we have coffee and fresh croissants. I am enjoying myself a bit too much.

We chug along quietly for the rest of the afternoon. We stop at dusk in another one of these little harbours that pepper the coast. Ned cooks sausages and mash for dinner. Then we have a few drinks, mainly in silence, looking out at the dark sea as the boat rocks quietly away.

I bed down for the night feeling quite worn out. My room is functional but cosy, with a bench bed and a squall of heavy blankets. A picture of a tall ship hangs on the wall, sails aloft. Not much else to report, but the whisky tastes great out here in the wilderness.

FRIENDS NOT YET MET

We start out early the next morning, before dawn's fingers have barely begun to stretch over the horizon. As pale light gently seeps into the darkness, we see a polar bear and her cub trundling along the coast. The mother looks thin. They break into a trot when they see us, as if glad for the company. It is a pleasant scene, but I am glad there is some distance between us. I'm reminded of a story from school about Captain Cook, or maybe Lord Nelson, beating a polar bear to death with nothing but an oar. I remember thinking that even back then there must have been a lot more people on earth than polar bears. He should have done the decent thing and sacrificed himself.

In the evening, we stop off at a small town. We eat fish and chips for dinner at a shabby little diner, just off the coast road. It turns out that we are close to a bar, one of the few in the area. We strike out, past the houses in the harbour nestled quietly together. Amber light leaks out of windows scattered here and there, and smoke rises from chimneys as their shadows grow fainter in the receding light. Darkness is once again king.

A winding road takes us upwards for a good twenty minutes before reaching a plateau, and there before us stands a ramshackle little building. I follow Ned in through a low door, and we both have to dip our heads on entering. It is a square room, divided by an isthmus of a bar, laden with upturned liquor bottles and optics.

There are maybe twenty people in here, huddled around the tables that are scattered, somewhat haphazardly, across a reddish-orange carpet. There are too many pictures on the walls, mainly old maps, and sepia-toned photographs of stern-looking men in sou'westers.

What light there is gives a rosy and welcoming glow to the faces of the patrons. They speak quietly among themselves and pay us scant attention. Several of the men at the bar give a nod at Ned, and he grunts and nods in recognition. They look like taciturn, hard-working men, with heavy beards and heavy shirts and heavy boots. A sign at the bar states, "Strangers are just friends you haven't met yet...best keep it that way".

Ned raises his chest as we approach the bar. A woman serving drinks glances over at us.

'Long-time no see Ned. You running another tour?' She has a wry smile, and a broad freckled face framed by a head of curly auburn hair.

'Howdy Ruthie,' says Ned, his voicing rising, 'that's right, I'm taking this gentleman, Mr Johns, to see the bay.'

'Hallo Mr Johns,' she says.

'Nice to meet you, please call me John.'

'Hallo John Johns. How are ya, my dear?'

'Very good thank you.'

She lifts a pint glass to a tap as she talks.

'You're lookin' well Ned, you been eating better since I last saw ya?'

'Well you know Ruthie, plenty busy, gotta' keep my energy up.'

'Has he been feeding ya right John?' Ruthie asks as she hands a pint of dark ale along the polished bar.

'Don't fall for that Saudi prince nonsense he comes out with. And be sure he doesn't give ya mackerel every day, he's got all sorts stashed away in that kitchen, enough to feed five Saudi princes,' she says, as she takes the money and turns to the till.

'Hush now Ruthie, you'll embarrass the gentleman,' Ned says as, as she turns back to us.

'Don't worry about me,' I say, laughing, 'we did have mackerel today. It was very reasonable.'

'The last tour he did, Japanese couple it was, poor sods, I bet ya they couldn't wait to get home and eat something different by the time they'd finished,' she says, chuckling to herself.

'Well now Ruthie, as a matter of fact, they sent me a card only last year and thanked me for the food y' hear,' Ned says in reply, almost blushing.

'Haha, I'm sure they did Ned. Anyway, what can I get you fellas?' she asks, looking at us directly, arms folded.

'A pint of that for me please,' I say, pointing at something that looks vaguely familiar. 'What will you have Ned?' I ask my companion.

'Give me the usual please Ruthie, and don't be stingy.'

We sit at one of the tables, silently enjoying the drinks and the warm hubbub of the bar, and observing the other patrons. They are in many ways just like the people at home, but at the same time, very different. It is hard to define. They look much the same, a bit heavier perhaps, and a bit hairier. But there is a difference that renders them at once mundane, and at the same time, quite exotic.

I am being lulled into tiredness by the gentle rhythms of the room. I am glad when Ned suggests going back to the boat. Just as we are saying goodbye to Ruthie, the main door swings open. In strides a large man who seems to take up most of the space in the room. He isn't dressed for the weather and looks out of place in a tatty tuxedo. He immediately moves towards us.

'Neddy boy, how are you doing?' he asks, smiling enthusiastically at my companion, and crouching slightly as he moves forward as if going in for a hug that fails to materialise. Ned raises an eyebrow.

'Not bad Jack, and you?' he says.

'Good, as ever, yes,' says the big man, as he continues into the room, greeting Ruthie and taking the time to smile or wave at several others in the room. He is tall and broad-shouldered, with wide features and a shock of blonde hair.

'Jack this is Mr Jo...,' starts Ned, before he is interrupted.

'Nice to meet you, Jim, how you doing? I'm Jack Grunbaum the Third, at your service. You're not from these parts, am I right?' he observes, with a friendly tone, and then focuses on me.

'Oh no, I'm from England,' I say, feeling like a rabbit caught in the headlights.

'England,' he says, smiling, 'oh great, yeah I have been there. It is close to Italy, am I right? I saw the prime minister on TV the other day. Have you met him Jim?'

'The prime minister?' I ask, perplexed. 'Well er, not in person.'

'Haha, not in person he says. That's just great,' replies the big man, still smiling. He then leans in conspiratorially:

'Most people round here Jim, they are a bit ignorant. I have been around. I know the Major of Newfoundland personally,' he says warmly, without arrogance, but as if he expects me to be impressed.

'Anyway,' he continues, turning to Ned, 'are you still running around in that beat-up old wreck Neddy?'

'She ain't so bad,' says Ned in response, lower lip jutting out slightly.

'You would have to drag me onto that boat with horses,' he says, laughing again and patting Ned on the back.

'Anyway Jim, I am sure it has been a pleasure, and for me too,' he says, turning to me and shaking my hand firmly. 'Neddy, see you again sometime buddy.'

And then he is gone, stalking further into the room where he quickly starts a new conversation.

We struggle back to the boat in the dark.

'So who was that?' I ask.

'That's Jack. He owns some of those houses down at the jetty. Thinks he's Donald Trump,' says Ned.

'Haha, more like Donald Duck in that outfit.'

Ned laughs at that, and we continue in silence.

At the boat, Ned further secures it to the jetty, and we retire to our cabins. I lie awake for some time, enjoying the rocking of the boat, and those sounds you only hear in harbours in the quiet of the night: the gentle knocking together of wood, the rattling of ropes and rings, furled canvass flapping in the breeze.

THE COLD COMETH

I wake in darkness, shivering. After an aeon, I summon the strength to reach over to the trunk by the bed and grab an extra blanket. A pale light outside the curtain catches my attention. Peering through I see the Milky Way, stretched across a pitch-black sky, like a vast string of celestial fairy lights. The whole world seems silent at that moment, except for the stars, which are so bright as to be almost blinding, and which seem to quiver with such a violence that, if closer, would surely also be deafening.

I lie awake for an hour or so, in awe, a small child again in a universe the scale of which I cannot begin to comprehend. I rise with the first light of the sun. Dawn's caresses bring little warmth, but they at least bring the comfort of company; Ned is up and together we silently prepare breakfast. The coffee is dark and strong and warms my bones, easing me back into the world. No wonder they drink so much of this stuff at the cold fringes of the earth.

Ned is distracted as we eat. He informs me that there have been storm warnings along the coast. He does not think it will affect us, but is monitoring the situation. The land is becoming more fragmented as we move north-west towards the Arctic Circle. Grey jagged rocks snarl at us from just below the surface of the water. Icebergs float past us, all in the same direction. A sense of desolation creeps over the boat, with both captain and passenger becoming subdued. I am adding layers of clothing as the temperature continues to drop.

Feeling bored, I set about exploring my surroundings. The boat is a trawler. It was built in 1964. Outside it is unkempt, but inside is a different matter, and the engine, a six-cylinder Chrysler motor, is well maintained, clean and oiled. Up top, there is a kitchen/dining area, and living quarters, two rooms that would accommodate maybe four people. There is also a large cupboard, which hides a mess of fishing gear. Down below, there is a functional bathroom and a small relaxation room with a bookcase and a comfy chair.

We don't stop for lunch today. I cook as we push on, Ned stays at the wheel, lost in concentration. We eat mackerel again, but this time with a pungent seaweed as accompaniment.

The afternoon is overcast and our mood follows. Ned steers silently whilst I grumble around the boat. We have started to act like an old couple. I try to sit out on the deck but the wind irks me. I go to the relaxing room and each configuration of blankets feels discomforting, and I rustle around like a dog in his basket, never quite finding the right spot. I move to the back of the boat and watch the white streaks left in our wake. We are about five days from our destination. I hope we can get some time on land before then.

THE DARKENING STORM

I am woken before sunrise by the starting of the motor. In semi-darkness, I stumble into the fore cabin and Ned is there, focused like a hawk. The storm warning has been increased and we are roughly equidistant between two harbours. Behind us, to the east, is the harbour where we visited the bar. Ahead, and some forty miles along the coast lies the next town. That is where Ned decides we are going. I make breakfast for both of us, but Ned barely registers, and I end up eating it all myself.

Dawn breaks slowly across the sky but fails to dispel fully the night. The boat is going faster than I have seen it go before. By lunchtime the waves have started to build, and there are black clouds rolling in from the north. To add to the general sense of unease, the icebergs are getting bigger, and portside it looks increasingly uninviting. Mid-afternoon, Ned slows the boat and starts looking to the land.

'We're not going to make harbour sir,' says Ned, soberly 'but we can't stay out at sea in this. I know a little cove not far from here where it might be safe to tie the boat up. It's a landward wind, so it won't be hard reachin' it - we just gotta make sure we hit the right bit of land.'

'Ok, what can I do,' I say, nervously.

'Pack a bag and sit tight,' he replies.

Ned steers the boat towards land, and heavy waves crash against our starboard side. Above us, the gods are growing fractious, and squalls of rain lash against the trawler. We jolt violently as the boat's underside meets firm land and grinds across it. I can hear the sound of wood being battered, I can taste salt and seaweed on my tongue, but my eyes are confounded, all is darkness, deep blue and indigoes, only the spray seems to carry a grey light.

The boat moves again. Ahead there is a small opening in the rocks. The engine thrums and strains as the waves grow fiercer and then we are through and into the cove. The wind subsides, the waves grow gentler, and the boat, still moving quickly, buffers into a bed of marshy polar reeds. We scrape against land again and thud to a halt.

Ned grabs a thick rope and jumps ashore, wrapping the middle of the rope around a large rock and digging the end, attached to something like a harpoon, into the ground. He does all this in driving black rain and I can only see him because of his bright orange jacket. He does the same at the back of the boat.

'We gotta' go now Mr Johns,' he says over the rising wind.

I follow Ned clumsily over the side of the boat. With a little help, I ease onto firm land, only for my feet to squelch into soggy marshland. I experience genuine fear for a moment as my boots sink and the ice-cold water seeps into them, but the ground holds firm. I say a quiet prayer of thanks for the fact that I brought a second stick. It is only a telescopic one, but using this and my sturdy wooden stick almost as crutches I am able to drag myself along at a fair pace. As we move away from the sea, towards sullen hills under an angry sky, I reflect, not for the first time, on the dangers of wishing. This is not quite what I meant by 'time on land'.

By midnight and Ned and I are huddled together in a small cavern, barely big enough for two, at the base of a string of sturdy dark hills. The pale light has been sucked out of the sky and replaced by leering, shifting blankets of thunder and shards of blinding pink lightning. A ferocious wind nips and bites every inch of body that is not covered by coat or blanket or hat. Despite the clamour outside, there is silence in our little receptacle of rock.

'Mr Johns, are you still awake?' Ned asks in the darkness.

'Yes Ned,' I say. 'Please call me John. I feel that now we have become better acquainted, it doesn't feel right that you call me Mr.'

'Ok John sir, will do.'

'By the way Ned,' I add.

'Yes, sir?'

'You smell worse close up.'

'Why thank you,' he responds, a little too jauntily for my liking, 'I did have a bath this year, which is one better than last year.'

'Well I should think myself lucky then,' I say.

'Did the Japanese tourists end up huddled together like this?' I ask.

'Nope,' he says in response.

'Lucky them.'

'Try and keep awake sir. I'd hate to have to kick you, but I will if y' start t' fall asleep. Don't want you catching hypothermia.'

'Have you been in this situation before?' I ask.

'Plenty,' he says, flatly.

'Ever lost anyone?' I ask, trying not to sound too concerned.

'Not yet,' he says, 'but I'm reckoning this might be how you want to go?'

'I didn't envisage freezing to death.'

'Don't worry 'bout that, the polar bears will get us before the cold,' he says, not at all comfortingly.

'Oh shit, really?' I ask, 'can we fight them? Have you got a gun?'

'Yep,' he says, pulling what looks like a rifle from a pouch strapped over his shoulder.

'Thank goodness. Is it possible to fight a polar bear without one? A famous explorer once did.' My teeth chatter as I say this, and my breath is a plume of white air.

'Ah, but you Brits are tough,' he says, looking over his gun and checking its sighting, 'it was likely a male at the end of the mating season. They're half dead through fightin' already. Easy pickins' for some puffed up ship's captain.'

'Really?' I say, my voice almost a squeak.

'Yep. It's the females you have to watch out fer.'

'Are there many around here?' I ask.

'Plenty.'

THE PADDING OF HEAVY FEET

It is about five in the morning. The sun has whipped a faint line on the horizon and the storm is easing. We are tired and silent. Ned thinks he has heard something snuffling about. I hear it too, a heavy sound...

'We gotta' move now,' he says, in hushed tones.

'What is it?' I whisper.

'A female. Let's go before she finds us.' At that, he rises to a crouch and beckons me out.

The rush you feel as you contemplate discovery by the world's largest land carnivore cannot be adequately conveyed in words. It is like a religious experience. It makes you wonder if those wildebeest are writhing around in throes of pain, or ecstasy, as the lions chomp into their necks. The blood sings, the heart does not merely race or pound, it grows wings and flies into the sky, leaving your empty shell flatfooted and pinned to the earth. It then rushes back into your body and every nerve, every capillary, explodes in agony. Time slows, everything becomes pin sharp. Then you move as if stepping on air.

We move in a state of grace, for what seems like forever: the universe has begun and ended before we have gone even five paces, thankfully in the right direction, as the snuffling sound recedes. Another expansion and contraction of the universe and we make it to a small clutch of trees. Turning, we see the silhouette of a polar bear, set against a deep blue canvas of indifferent and immobile stars. She is on four legs, still snuffling around, close to the cave. She sniffs, and stands to her full height, ten, twelve, a thousand feet, and lets out a roar of warning. With that, she turns and vanishes from the horizon, her cub trundling along after her. We are frozen in place. Eventually, Ned stands, rifle in hand. I'm not sure it would have done any good.

Still alert, we move softly, stealthily, or so it seems, in the direction of the boat. Before my heart has had a chance to slow though, another sound starts, a barking, close by. Ned turns and takes us to a narrow crack in some standing rocks. He motions me in first, crouches in front of me, rifle poised.

The barking grows near. It is ferocious, worse than the polar bear. I think again about our ancestors, left out to die. What must the first bite feel like? How many bites till you die? Do they kill you quickly or do they just tuck in as a pack? What must it feel like to feel your intestines being chewed on whilst still alive? These unhelpful thoughts take but a second to flit back and forth in my brain, before the sound is no longer somewhere else, it is there, in front of us. Looking over Ned's shoulder, I see one, two, three sets of bright blue eyes and bared teeth. I can almost smell the foul breath of the beasts as they lurch and strain towards us. My heart soars, it has left the bounds of the earth, it has broken the constraints of gravity, it flies now through the brightening sky, across the great ribbon of the Milky Way, no longer separate from, but part of, this great cacophony of light and sound. At last, I am going home.

'That you Ned?' a voice says from the other side of the rock.

'Howdy Ruthie, what took y' so long?'

'Some old fool thought he could beat the storm. Went the wrong direction.'

I am shaken from a state of near ecstasy, by a large tongue, that makes its way slowly from my chin up the side of my face. The blue eyes that moments earlier seemed primed to eat me, are now plaintive. I stroke the deep fur and feel a profound sense of relief. The short ride back to the boat is bumpy but I barely notice. My first and probably last sled ride, pulled along by eight noisy huffing barking huskies.

At the boat, another surprise: Donald Duck, still in his tatty tuxedo, heaving with all of his strength, to get the heavily listing boat upright in the water.

'Neddy, so glad you're okay buddy.'

'Jack,' says Ned, nodding at the other man, 'mighty appreciative of y' both comin.'

'We're not going to let you go down in this old bucket just yet.' says the large man in response.

Both men smile at each other warmly and shake hands.

'Ok fellas, enough of the love-in, we got a boat to fix.'

The boat is fine, some damage to the paddles but nothing that can't be fixed. I am sent, only half-reluctantly, to bed. I promptly collapse, and sleep soundly for several hours, though I am always dimly aware of clanking sounds and the voices of three people working in very cold conditions to fix a storm-damaged boat.

A QUIET HARBOUR

By the time I wake the next day, Ruthie, Jack, and the dogs have gone, and the boat is on its way. The sky is clear, and dawn has replaced the brooding clouds, with flecks of bright yellow. The mood onboard has brightened. Despite the storm, we have made good time, and our estimated time of arrival is three days. This gives me plenty of time to enjoy what remains of the journey.

I do a bit of line fishing in the afternoon and catch a couple of hakes. Ned does indeed have a well-stocked kitchen, and that evening I bake fish in mustard sauce, with pickled cucumbers and potatoes, sautéed in fish stock.

Portside, the landscape is changing as we edge alongside the Torngat National Park, a vast mountainous area, rich in lush greens and browns. In the afternoon, we see another polar bear, gambolling with her cub. She looks well-fed and we slow the boat up to watch for a while. The post-storm sky is clear, and as darkness falls, the northern lights are faintly visible.

We settle into another little natural harbour and sit out on the deck, wrapped up, with an excellent bourbon for company and some hot chocolate on the side.

'So what made y' decide to come out here again?' Ned asks.

'I had the idea that it was time for me to die,' I say, feeling foolish.

'Are y' still of that opinion?' he asks.

'Well clearly last night I wasn't,' I say. 'I know it must seem childish. I just feel old and tired, and I don't wish to end my days in a nursing home.'

'It's prob'ly no worse than the alternatives,' he says, sipping from his glass.

'What are the alternatives?' I ask, looking skywards.

'Well s' pose y' could finish yourself off, like hanging, or maybe jump off a building. That's gotta' hurt though. Could have an accident – that's gonna' hurt too. Might be murdered. Or y' could die on your feet, takin' packs of food onto an oil rig.' His brow furrows as he says this.

'Is that how you're going to go?' I ask.

'Probl'y.'

'That doesn't sound too bad,' I muse, still looking up at the sky, the stars becoming more visible as my eyes adjust to the darkness.

'Better 'n an old folks' home I guess.'

'An old neighbour of mine died at home,' I say, 'on his settee, reading a book. I found him. The book was open, and his reading glasses were on the floor next to his body. He looked so peaceful.'

'What was the book?' Ned asks.

'It was called 'How to stay young,'' I say.

We both laugh.

'Actually it wasn't,' I say, feeling a stab of shame. 'I forget what it was called, but it was a rather sad book, about some people stuck on a boat in the ocean who turn to cannibalism. Oh god…'

'Don't worry, I won't be eating y' any time soon,' says Ned. 'Reckon y'd taste pretty bad, although some of that mustard sauce might help.'

'Thanks.'

'My wife died last year,' I say, 'and I've not really got over it. I've got two grown-up children, but they're busy with their own lives, and I find them a bit annoying to be honest.'

'Yep,' says Ned.

'I've got two lovely grandchildren, though. How about you?' I ask.

'Nope.'

'Ever been married?'

'Three times,' says Ned, flatly.

'Three times, wow. How did that happen?'

'Well, the first one still lives round here, she's a proud woman, I was kind of an asshole. The second one, she's over in Montreal. A bit of a mean girl that one.' As he speaks, Ned looks now at the sea, into the darkness. The waves lap against the side of the boat.

'…and the third…?' I ask, tentatively.

'Emmy,' he says, smiling, 'she was kind, funny, bossy, and real sweet.'

'So where is she now?' I ask.

Ned takes a long sip of his drink.

'She died,' he says, matter-of-factly, still looking out to sea.

'Her boat sunk, over at Manitoba. She was expectin' our first child.'

'Shit, I'm sorry,' I say, stricken.

'Was it you sank the boat?'

'No of course not, but I'm here complaining,' I say, 'at least I had a life with my wife.'

'Yeah well, you're the one out here lookin' to die,' he says, with a shrug. 'I'm happy.'

'I'm sorry anyway.'

'Yep.'

'So what y' gonna do when we get there?' Ned asks, changing the subject.

'I'm not sure,' I say. 'I used to read maps when I was a kid. I used to imagine what it would be like, to sail into the bay on a bright winter morning. Did you know it is the second biggest bay in the world? I suppose I'll decide what to do next once we arrive.'

'We ain't there yet. Plenty of wolves and bears between here and there. Some mighty big fish too.'

I laugh. Ned looks up at the sky one more time and rises. 'Anyways, night John, see you in the morning.'

AN UNEXPECTED DIVERSION

The next morning is exceptionally clear. Dawn came whilst I slept and painted the world a brighter hue. I am greeted by the smell of fried bacon and fresh coffee. The sea is clear and choppy, and salty spray leaps up as the boat cuts through the waves.

We are approaching a spike on the map, rounding Torngat and sailing into the bay of Ungava, a particularly barren looking area. This means that we are leaving Labrador and entering Nunavik, which, according to my guidebook, has a predominantly Inuit population, scattered throughout the small towns and villages along the coast.

As we follow the coastline, the landscape becomes bleaker. Towards the end of the afternoon, as the sun starts to set, we slow down. Ned turns the boat towards land, and into a small harbour. A man on the jetty sees us, waves and walks to meet us.

The boat clunks into place. Ned clambers down and briskly hops onto the jetty. The stranger moves towards him and they shake hands warmly.

'Ainngai Ned, Takunahaarnakuni. Qanuitpin?' The stranger asks.

'Ainngai Marcelle, Qaniungi,' says Ned, in the same language.

The stranger is tall and long-limbed and wearing a bright yellow jacket. He looks at me warmly.

'Marcelle, this is Mr Johns,' says Ned, smiling.

'Mr Johns, I am Marcelle. Tunngahugit!'

'Tunngahugit is welcome in Inuit John,' says Ned.

'Thank you, nice to meet you,' I say. 'Please call me John.'

I step gingerly off the boat onto the jetty. Marcelle reaches his hand out and we shake.

'How has your journey been John? You had a problem with the weather, no?' he asks me.

'We did get caught up in that storm. We had a few shaky moments, but survived.'

This unplanned interlude leaves me feeling bemused, as Ned and Marcelle walk away together speaking animatedly. I follow them into a grey concrete building. Inside it is cold and the air is damp and salty. Maps of coastal areas cover the walls and sophisticated looking equipment – computers, radio, what looks like sonar, adorn several long desks.

'Coffee, monsieur?' asks Marcelle.

'Yes sure, thanks,' I say, blankly.

'Sorry John.' says Ned, seeming more relaxed than I have seen him on the trip so far, 'Marcelle is my brother in law. Ex-brother in law.'

'Oh, which wife?' I say.

'The mean one.'

Marcelle looks serious for a moment, rests his hand on Ned's shoulder, and laughs.

'Ah, Ned is too harsh, my sister is not too bad. She just takes a bit of getting used to.'

'I tried for five years,' says Ned, as he appraises the room.

'Where's Aula?' he asks.

'At this moment, she is fixing a mechanical fault with the damn generator. The storm knocked something out: I do not know what, I'm a lawyer, I know nothing about damn mechanics!'

I look at him blankly.

'Aula is my wife, John,' he says, 'she will be back soon and then we will eat. I have prepared something very special.'

Still somewhat disoriented, and carrying a very hot cup of coffee, I follow them into a larger adjoining building. The space here is much cosier. There are deep rugs on the floor and hangings on the walls depicting seals, bears, and birds as well as people in canoes. Another door, at the far side of the room, suggests a kitchen. Marcelle beckons us over to a heavy wooden table, and we sit down. The coffee is thick and bitter. Marcelle is clearing the table when the door to the kitchen opens and a woman walks in, accompanied by a sudden draft of steam and heat. She moves with a grace that seems at odds with the dark blue oily overalls she wears. She looks tired but smiles at us warmly.

'Ned, how nice to see you,' she speaks softly and focuses her gaze intently at him.

'Aula,' Ned says, beaming, and they embrace.

'Oh you are always early,' she says warmly, 'I wanted to get changed before you arrived.'

Marcelle snorts. 'Do not worry my love, you are just as lovely in overalls!'

'Pfft!' she says, 'and you have company?'

'Yep, this is Mr Johns.'

'How nice to meet you, Mr Johns. Are you from England?' She holds out her hand and looks straight at me. Her face is broad and framed by cropped black hair, flecked with grey. I stand and shake her hand

'Please call me John. Yes I am, from Somerset, in the south-west of England.'

'Cheddar cheese!' she sings with delight.

'Ha, yes indeed, I live quite close to the gorge.'

'How lovely,' she smiles, 'well please excuse me, John, I must have a wash and change.'

She leaves the room and the three of us sit for a moment, quietly regarding her absence.

Ned breaks the silence. 'So what slush are y' cooking us tonight Marcelle, something French?'

'Not quite my friend, how could I possibly outdo myself since the last time you visited us? Tonight I am preparing food from the land of my wife. We will eat Murktuk,' he says, with a triumphant smile, then leans towards us and whispers, 'something of a delicacy in these parts.'

'You're serving us whale skin?' asks Ned, sounding indignant.

'Not just any whale skin, sliced and fried whale skin,' he says, with relish, 'the likes of which you have never tasted before.'

After this, we are shown to our rooms and take some time to relax. I have my first shower since leaving Montreal. The water is very cold. It takes me back to the days when Laura and I would go camping. We would rise early, when the grass was still wet, and brush our teeth in darkness. Then we would go walking, around the great ranges of Europe; the Alps, the Pyrenees, the Dolomites. We would return in darkness, and sleep the kind of deep, dark sleep that is only possible after long days outdoors. My room is cosy, and I doze for an hour or so, thinking on these happy memories.

Later that evening, we sit down to eat. A salty fish broth is served first, it is deep and rich. This is followed by strips of what I take to be whale meat, and the tastiest chips I have ever eaten.

Aula speaks first:

'So John, what brings you to this place, so far north? Are you working?'

'Oh no, I'm just a tourist.' My voice cracks a little as I say this. Is that all I am? What about my plan? Surely, this trip ranks me above the common or garden tourist, I wonder.

'Like Sanjuro and Motoko?' asks Marcelle, his eyes brightening.

'You mean the Japanese tourists?' I ask.

'Oh yes,' says Aula, 'they were so lovely. He was a cetacean scientist if I remember, and she was...a writer?'

'A journalist,' says Ned, 'They were interested in the migration routes. We followed some humpbacks from Ungava to the bay and round...'

'Ah those unfortunate people,' says Marcelle, grinning, 'all they ate was fish every day. Not sushi John,' he says, beaming, 'just Ned's mackerel!'

Ned sighs. 'Here we go again, Ruthie was peddling the same lies earlier. Don't forget who cooked whale skin tonight.'

'Oh, Ruthie. How is she?' asks Aula.

'Same as ever,' says Ned, sheepishly.

'Ned's first wife,' says Marcelle, still with a mischievous grin on his face.

'You kept that quiet Ned,' I splutter. Before this line of conversation has time to develop, however, Ned has redirected us.

'He came here to die Aula.'

'Is that true John?' Aula asks, looking surprised.

'Thanks Ned,' I reply, ruefully. 'Well I erm, I don't know what to say. I'm coming to the end of my life. I feel tired. I always had this dream to come here, and I kind of imagined that I would…meet God somewhere along the way, and that would be that.'

'In this god-forsaken wilderness, you'd be lucky!' says Marcelle, dramatically.

'Marcelle please,' says Aula, chiding her husband. 'But John, did you imagine that you could set a time and place on such a thing?'

'Hmm yes, a bit presumptuous I know,' I say in reply.

'And you are so healthy, you do not look like you are ready to die.'

'That's what I said,' Ned chirps.

'Yes but I feel like it,' I say. 'I feel tired. I am seventy-one Aula, do you know how many days and nights that is? Everyone goes on about how great it is that we are all living longer. But no one asked *us* if we want to live longer. Do I have to go on forever?'

'You should have seen him when he thought he was gonna' be eaten by wolves though Aula. He changed his mind quick-sharpish then,' says Ned, eyes on the food as he tucks into a chunk of whale skin.

'Ha, it's true,' I reply.

'Well John,' says Aula, pausing briefly, 'if you will forgive me for being rude, but people around here do not have time to get tired. They go on until they drop dead. But when you see the old ones, their lives are hard, but their eyes are bright, and their spirits are strong. It is the daily fight that makes them so. Perhaps you just need a bit more…discomfort in your life?'

'How do I do that?' I ask. 'Do I just give away all of my possessions and become a tramp? I can't get work, nobody would have me, I'm too old. And I have a comfortable pension, which I worked hard for.'

'I understand, John,' she says. 'It is a paradox. We must all of us give in to entropy eventually; just some go more quickly than others.'

'Bah!' says her husband, chewing on a strip of beef, 'that is a typical engineer thing to say, John. Ignore her, she has no grasp of beauty!'

'Ah you French fool!' says his wife in response, waving him away with her hand.

Not wanting to talk all night about myself, or our collective dooms, I change the subject.

'So what's your story?' I ask.

'Me?' says Aula.

'Both of you.'

'I was born in Quebec,' says Aula, 'but my family are all over Manitoba and Nunavik; I have a lot of nephews and nieces. I coordinate meteorological observations for the Nunavik area.'

'Wow,' I say, 'how did you get into that?'

'I always enjoyed fixing things, just like my dad, so I became an engineer. It's not so exciting most of the time, but it has its moments. And he...keeps me company,' she says, wrinkling her nose and turning to look at Marcelle.

'Pah!' says her husband, in mock outrage. 'I am from the north of France but moved to Canada as a child. I'm a lawyer by trade. I came up here from Montreal during the Oka crisis in 1989. The government was trying to build a golf course over lands belonging to the Oka Mohawk people. It turned into a nasty confrontation, the whole world was watching,' he says, theatrically, as if addressing a courtroom. 'Aula's father was one of the original warriors who set up the barricades. They were being charged with criminal activity. I wounded up helping to defend him and half the Mohawk nation.' He looks at his wife. 'And then I met Aula and became bound to this place. Now I do nothing but read, cook and help her fix her damn machinery.'

I laugh at their story, and Marcelle's telling of it.
'You both seem very happy. By the way, this food is delicious. The whale meat is amazing. And the chips are fantastic.'
'Thank you,' says Marcelle, beaming. 'I must say, I did not take to the dish at first. It seemed too strong in flavour, and fatty. But the more I ate of it, the more I understood its subtlety. I miss French beef though...'

he says, a wistful light in his eyes…then stands with a start.

'Desert!' he exclaims, and dashes through the door, emerging again with a large silver plate.

'Baked Alaska!' he shouts triumphantly and begins to spoon it into each of our dishes.

'What do you think Ned?' asks Aula as we eat. Ned looks surprised to be asked, and is more concerned with his desert.

'I said my piece Aula, I will go when I go, probably on my feet. I would hate to rot away in one o' those homes they have. Give me a freezing sea any day.'

STRONG COFFEE

Dawn has slid her icy fingers across the land well before I wake the next morning. It takes me half an hour to prise myself out from under a stack of heavy blankets. I find my way to the kitchen and after a few minutes fumbling around, I put a pot of coffee on the stove.

Despite the temperature, it is sunny outside, and I bask in the yellow light that streams through the window. Looking out, I feel a great sense of loss. I breathe. Ahead of me is a magnificent white vista. Part of me yearns to stay here in this wilderness: the emptiness, the desolation, is extremely inviting. And yet, I think of my house in London for the first time in weeks. I think of George, my grandson. I have watched him grow, from a wee speck of a thing into such a funny little boy, always making everybody laugh. My journey's end is fast approaching, and I have no idea what is waiting for me. Increasingly though, I think it is unlikely to be God, or the sharp tearing grasp of a wolf pack.

'John, would you help me please?' says Aula, as she walks into the room, heavily wrapped in a thick hooded coat.
'Sure Aula. What with?' I say in response.
'The generator has stopped again,' she says, ruefully.
'Is that why it's so cold?' I ask.
'Yes. And those fools drank too much last night, I cannot rouse Marcelle. You must be a hardened drinker.'
'Ha no, I'm a lightweight I'm afraid. Coffee is my vice, would you like one?' I ask.
'After we fix the generator.'
'Ok, what can I do?'

The generator is located in a shed, behind the main building. Unfortunately, it is out of the morning sun. I spend half an hour holding cables, whilst Aula works away with assorted spanners. I notice her hands, the skin is hard and windblown, and her fingernails are thick and layered. At one point, she is on her back under the generator, loosening a bolt, when her hand slips off and cracks against the cold hard metal. She swears and her face creases into a frown.

'Do you really want to die, John?' she asks, still working away.

'I don't know Aula, I'm just bored, and I miss my wife. I sit at home, I go out, I do this, I do that. It is boring. It is…worse than death.'

'Well do something else then. Don't waste your precious time. My grandma died when she was only sixty-one. She created this wonderful sense of cosiness, John, of comfort. When she died, she left such a big hole in all of our lives.'

'I won't leave much of a hole I'm afraid, I don't bring much comfort!'

'Well, you must change that then. Do not sit back. Go and make sure you will be missed. If you can do this, you won't want to die so easily, you will cling to every day.'

Back in the kitchen, Marcelle has made coffee, thick black warming coffee that makes me think of Nordic fishermen, dressing silently in the dark mornings, sipping grumpily on their sweetened tar, before giving themselves over to the sea, in search of sustenance. Do they ever meet God, I wonder.

Before setting off, we load various items on to the boat. The straps on the tarpaulin are as hard as ice, they freeze the bones of my fingers and snap against the skin. When we leave, it feels like I am leaving old friends. Marcelle and Aula embrace both of us. As the vessel chugs off, I envy them their quiet life here, but not perhaps the cold mornings, or the dodgy generator.

PLACE THAT SMELLS OF ROTTEN MEAT

Dawn's golden yellow fingers streak across the northern sky as the boat chugs onwards. Not far to go now, in fact, we have entered the Hudson Straits. The water here is calmer and eases the boat's progress as if we are being gently pushed along by some invisible force.

Mid-morning, we enter the bay. This is what I had dreamed of, this coming into the bay. I pictured a grey mist hanging over a vast silent body of water. I imagined the boats along the shore, gently rocking to and fro', great gulls cawing at each other through the mists. The sun's rays would peek through, and then, like the first men, I would gaze upon pristine beauty. Instead, I am greeted by bright sunshine, and an old man in a stained vest. I cannot even tell we are in a bay. There is land off to the left but we keep clear because of the rocks, and to the right, it is just open water. We could be tootling along the British south coast in winter. There is a lovely tang in the air though, and lots of birds, albeit somewhat smaller, and less majestic, than I'd imagined.

The boat continues without event. Realising my journey is nearing some kind of conclusion, I pack my suitcase and sit on the bed for a while. It feels extremely cosy and safe, out here in the wilderness, with only an old mattress and the soft chugging engine of the Santiago. The sun is warming the sides of the boat.

'John, you gotta' come out here,' calls Ned, his voice ringing out over the rhythmic sound of the engine

'What's happening?' I ask.

'You gotta' be on deck right now. This is the sweet spot,' he says, with a note of excitement in his voice.

I stumble out. The deck feels solid. The air is briny.

'What is it?' I say.

'Look over there.'

I follow his pointing finger across the bay. Portside, the land is becoming clearly defined. A flock of white birds moves purposefully overhead. I can see a small habitation, some boats, some buildings, even a small church. To starboard side, over in the distance, a sliver of green shows for the first time that we are in a bay.

Something comes over me then, and I sit. The boat glides across the face of the water. I feel more at peace than I have ever felt. It is, for a moment, exquisite.

'You still alive John?' asks Ned.

'Yes thanks,' I say.

'How's God doin'?' he asks.

'He's fine, thank you,' I say in reply.

'Good good, how 'bout some coffee?' he asks. Of course, I would love a coffee, I think, and say so.

Puvirnituq is a small town. Its name means 'place where there is a smell of rotten meat', which seems a bit unfair. The town is unprepossessing it must be said, and quite grey. Faded shops stand blankly with their shutters half-open. People buy hardware. Cars beep.

A bus full of schoolchildren brings a sudden flash of noise, and colour, as it trundles past, the windows full of smiles and woolly hats. It feels odd to be back in civilisation, after my time on the boat, and a bit disappointing. The whole place seems to rock gently. We get a quick bite at a little deli, before returning to the boat and continuing our journey.

Churchill on the west of the bay is bigger than Purvirnituq and is our final destination. It takes us the better part of the morning to get there. We leave the coastline for the first time, to scoot across the bay's silvery waters. When we arrive, it seems less a town than an industrial port, and we park the boat in a vast yard made up of innumerable jetties. Even out here on the edge of the world, humankind is industrious.

'So what y' gonna do now?' Ned asks as we walk along the shore into town.

'I'm not sure,' I answer.

'Y' really gonna stay here?' he asks.

'Possibly for a day or two, but after that, I don't know.'

'Well I'll be stayin' over tonight,' he says, 'then I'm gonna' load her up and head back east. Might even take the boat 'round Labrador and up the Hudson to Montreal. It would be hard goin', but there's some great scenery on the way. I do reasonable rates for passengers.'

I follow him into a peeling, windblown diner. The warmth hits us as we walk in, and the smell of crispy fries and coffee assails our senses.

'That sounds like a good plan,' I say, smiling and feeling suddenly caught up in the warmth, the smell and the sounds of the place, at once familiar and at the same time, entirely exotic.

'I will let you know.'

Churchill

Hudson Bay

Canada

Dearest Monica and Matthew,

I am sorry for all the cloak and dagger stuff. I am in Canada, I have missed you all terribly. I will be travelling by boat to Montreal over the next two weeks, so probably won't be in touch. I will fly home from there but will call once I have booked a flight. Sorry if I panicked you, I hope that you can forgive me.

See you all soon,

Lots of love

Dad xxx

EPILOGUE

I worry about those I love dying. Beneath this anxiety lies something equally unsettling, veiled and lurking just out of reach – the knowledge I too will die one day.

Maybe it's only when confronted with our imminent demise that most of us realise or acknowledge this hidden truth, and even then, we only see it dimly, unaware of its vast terrain and the hold it has over us.

I was tired of life, of myself, and of grief. I see now that I was mourning Laura, but also our life together, and grieving for my own mortality. I have also discovered, or remembered, that the world is bigger than I can possibly imagine, and life is hard for most of the creatures, human and animal, that live on it. Good and kind people can be found most places though, if you take the time to look for them, or are lucky enough to find them.

Death is inevitable, but there is a great deal else about life that is not, albeit sometimes it is maddening, painful or sad. Life can also be funny, surprising, exhilarating. In trying to acknowledge our impending non-existence, we can perhaps taste more fully the sweetness of life and bear its bitterness with a lighter heart. The stars may be indifferent to our small fates, but we do not have to be.

THE END

Tokyo

Dear Ned,

    We send you warm greetings from Tokyo. We hope that you are well. The enclosed photograph is one we took on the journey – do you remember that day? We are so grateful to you and have never forgotten your kindness and hospitality. We would like again to one day visit you, and this time if we are very lucky you might honour us by cooking your famous swan ☺

Wishing you health and longevity

Motoko and Sanjuro Kujiro

A note from the author

I hope you like my book. Thank you for reading it. If you enjoyed it, would you be doing me a great service by reviewing it on Amazon. And I'd love to hear from you in person too - please feel free to drop me a line.

Acknowledgements

Thank you to those wonderful people who read versions of this story, including my mum, Judy, Ralf, Nat and Liam. Thank you not just for reading my story but for your encouragement, kind words, suggestions, and constructive criticism. Thank you also to my wonderful girls, Linh and Violet, and especially to Anh, who was my first and most enthusiastic reader.

About the author

Peter Traynor lives in Leeds, UK with his wife, daughters and a relentless rabbit. He would love to write more fiction and is already thinking of a series of short stories set in ancient Britain. If you would like to know more about the author, or contact him, please go to gmadlife.com.

Images

Front cover photograph: © Anna Om, *Amazing landscape of beautiful bright milky way*. iStock Photos.

Back cover photograph: © Adventure Photo, Forest Silhouette and Milky Way Astrophotography Landscape. iStock Photos.

Whale photo: CC Brigitte Werner, *Humpback whale breaching*.
https://pixabay.com/de/users/werner22brigitte-5337/

Printed in Dunstable, United Kingdom